Captain Kidd: Pirate Hunter

by Damian Harvey and Peter Cottrill

This is a story about Captain Kidd, but he was a real person. He was asked to hunt pirates by King William II of England, but was hanged for piracy in 1701. No one really knows whether he was a pirate, or a pirate hunter. There are many tales of the treasure he buried, which was never found.

First published in 2010 by
Franklin Watts
338 Euston Road
London NW1 3BH

Franklin Watts Australia
Level 17/207 Kent Street
Sydney NSW 2000

Text © Damian Harvey 2010
Illustrations © Peter Cottrill 2010

The rights of Damian Harvey to be identified as the author
and Peter Cottrill as the illustrator of this Work have been asserted
in accordance with the Copyright, Designs and Patents Act, 1988.

A CIP catalogue record for this book is available
from the British Library.

ISBN 978 0 7496 9439 5 (hbk)
ISBN 978 0 7496 9445 6 (pbk)

Series Editor: Jackie Hamley
Series Advisor: Catherine Glavina
Series Designer: Peter Scoulding

Printed in China

Franklin Watts is a division of
Hachette Children's Books,
an Hachette UK company
www.hachette.co.uk

Long ago, I was a cabin boy for Captain Kidd. People said he was a pirate, but I think he was the bravest captain in England.

At that time, the seas were full
of terrifying pirates. Somebody
had to stop them.

The King of England sent
for Captain Kidd.
"Hunt down these pirates and
make the seas safe!" he ordered.

We set sail in a huge ship with a splendid crew who hated the thieving pirates.

Our adventure started well.

But a few days later, lots of our crew
were rude to some important people.

They were
taken away
to be
punished.

We had to sail across the ocean without them. But Captain Kidd would not give up. "We'll find a new crew," he declared.

When we arrived in New York,
many men wanted to join us.
"Big rewards for finding stolen
treasure!" cried Captain Kidd.

I didn't like the new crew at all –
they looked more like pirates than
pirate hunters.

We sailed for many months
without spotting a single pirate.

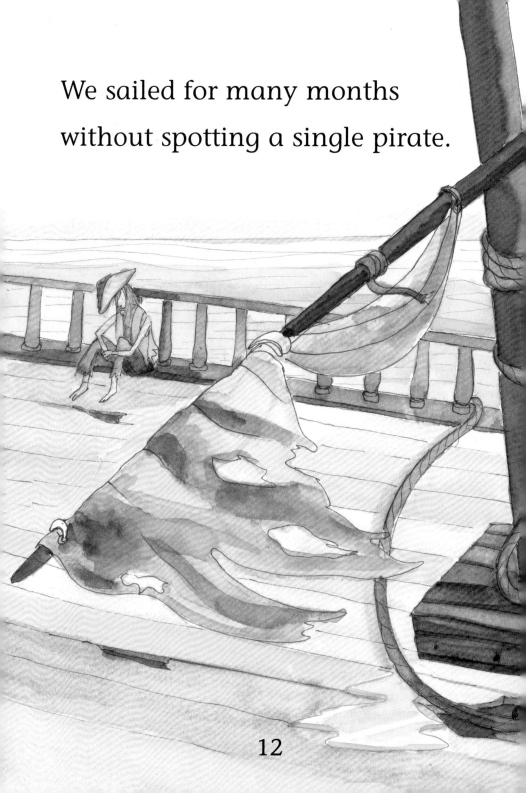

Our ship began to leak and the crew grew tired, hungry and sick.

Finally, we spotted a ship.

"Attack!" shouted the crew.

"No!" cried Captain Kidd.

"That's not a pirate ship. We're
not pirates, we hunt pirates."
The crew was furious.

Then we spotted a bigger ship.
"Pirates ahoy!" shouted
Captain Kidd. "Attack!"

The huge ship was full of gold and jewels, silks and furs, spices and salt. "We'll get a big reward for this!" cried Captain Kidd.

But the crew started sharing
the treasure between them.
Captain Kidd and I hid as
much as we could ...

... then we found out that the ship wasn't a pirate ship at all!

"Everyone hand back the treasure immediately!" Captain Kidd ordered.

But the crew laughed and sailed on.

Soon after that, we spotted
a real pirate ship.
"Attack!" shouted Captain Kidd.
The crew refused.

"We're pirates now, not pirate hunters," they yelled, forcing us to hide in the captain's cabin.

As our ship was leaking, lots of the crew joined the pirate ship. We sailed slowly back to New York.

Captain Kidd knew he'd be in trouble. He hoped his friends in England would help him.

He didn't want anyone stealing
the treasure in his cabin, so he
sent some away ...

… and buried some secretly.

When we got to New York,
Captain Kidd was thrown
into prison for being a pirate.

Most of his treasure was found
quickly, but not all of it.

No one knew where Captain Kidd
hid the rest of his treasure ...

... no one except me!

Puzzle 1

Put these pictures in the correct order.
Which event do you think is most important?
Now try writing the story in your own words!

Puzzle 2

1. England's ships need your help!

2. I hid his treasure map.

3. Give that treasure back!

4. I order you to stop these pirates.

5. He was the best captain on the seas.

6. My friends will help me to get out of prison.

Choose the correct speech bubbles for the characters above. Can you think of any others? Turn over to find the answers.

Answers

Puzzle 1

The correct order is: 1d, 2b, 3c, 4a, 5f, 6e

Puzzle 2

Captain Kidd: 3, 6

Tom (cabin boy): 2, 5

King of England: 1, 4

Look out for more Hopscotch Adventures:

Aladdin and the Lamp
ISBN 978 0 7496 6692 7

Blackbeard the Pirate
ISBN 978 0 7496 6690 3

George and the Dragon
ISBN 978 0 7496 6691 0

Jack the Giant-Killer
ISBN 978 0 7496 6693 4

Beowulf and Grendel
ISBN 978 0 7496 8551 5*
ISBN 978 0 7496 8563 8

Agnes and the Giant
ISBN 978 0 7496 8552 2*
ISBN 978 0 7496 8564 5

The Dragon and the Pudding
ISBN 978 0 7496 8549 2*
ISBN 978 0 7496 8561 4

Finn MacCool and the Giant's Causeway
ISBN 978 0 7496 8550 8*
ISBN 978 0 7496 8562 1

Blackbeard's End
ISBN 978 0 7496 9437 1*
ISBN 978 0 7496 9443 2

Pirate Jack and the Inca Treasure
ISBN 978 0 7496 9438 8*
ISBN 978 0 7496 9444 9

Pirates of the Storm
ISBN 978 0 7496 9440 1*
ISBN 978 0 7496 9446 3

TALES OF SINBAD THE SAILOR

Sinbad and the Ogre
ISBN 978 0 7496 8559 1*
ISBN 978 0 7496 8571 3

Sinbad and the Whale
ISBN 978 0 7496 8553 9*
ISBN 978 0 7496 8565 2

Sinbad and the Diamond Valley
ISBN 978 0 7496 8554 6*
ISBN 978 0 7496 8566 9

Sinbad and the Monkeys
ISBN 978 0 7496 8560 7*
ISBN 978 0 7496 8572 0

For more Hopscotch Adventures and other Hopscotch books, visit:
www.franklinwatts.co.uk

* hardback